Deidra's Love
By
KeKe Renée

Latest Releases

By Keke Renée:

Wet Heat

His Peace, Her Pleasure

Baby, It's Cold Outside

Love Don't Live Here Anymore, Book 1, 2

Every Time We Touch (A Wet Heat Novelette)

One Night Only-A Novelette Book 1

Cassian and Savannah Love By Design Book 2

Upcoming 2020/2021

Seeking in Romance (Touch,Bare, Please,Love)

Haven

Protecting Bria

Dedication

I want to thank, first and foremost, God, for giving me the strength to keep pursuing my dreams and goals. My mom and big brother. My niece and nephew, and to all of my cousins. Especially a huge thanks to my family in heaven: Grandmother, Aunt, Father. You are always with me no matter where I go, and everything you've taught me has made me a better person.

Introduction

This is a continuation of One Night Only, a novelette of a workplace, enemies-to-lovers romance. Love By Design will leave you wanting more. I won't give too much away, but you'll have to follow and subscribe to my newsletter for sneak peeks, updates, and cover reveals for more details.

Are you signed up for my newsletter?

Join today and find out all the latest in new releases, contests, giveaways, sneak peeks and more.

https://landing.mailerlite.com/webforms/landing/r7j2s6

Author's Note:

Deidra Simmons first appears in Cassian and Savannah: Love by Design. You do not need to read the series to follow this new story, but some of the characters will make a brief appearance in Deidra's story.

Synopsis:

A girl can only work hard, dream big, and stay focused on getting to the top for so long until she realizes becoming a partner of a top entertainment law firm may not be the dream job she thought it would be after all. The closer I get to achieving my dream, the easier my world starts to unravel, and what I didn't expect was the chaos to come in the sinful package of Logan Nash. My boss's son and my top rival for becoming partner in the firm, he tests my every decision. It doesn't help that we're enemies with a mutual competition in the workplace and outside. Logan is living the life he's wanted since he was young: a high-profile position at his father's firm, unlimited money, and an endless stream of women. He didn't expect to fall for me, a sassy, curvy, uptight virgin who pushes his every button.

Chapter 1: Deidra

"Savannah, let me call you back; I'm just walking into the office now… Okay, dinner later today sounds good." I hung up the call, stepping on the elevator and hitting number twelve for my floor. I sighed as the doors were about to close with me being the only person inside, which I loved because I could gather my thoughts before I hit the ground running to get the day started. But when I began to do just that, a hand stopped the doors from closing, and a man stepped into the enclosure, hitting the button for the fifteenth floor.

He stood toward the door wearing shades, probably still drunk from a night of excessive partying. *Who wears shades at nine in the morning?* I thought to myself. The dark blue suit fit him, showing off his broad shoulders and muscular build. I'd say he was around six-one or six-two, with an olive skin tone and strong jawline with a cleft chin. To the women who probably fall at his feet for his slicked-back dark hair and long nose, full lips, and goatee, he'd be perfect. For me, I'd pass on that pretty boy type or what I like to call the "man whore club," whom I avoided getting involved with because I didn't chase after men. I served class and not drama when it came to men. Finally, the elevator stopped on my floor, and I stepped right past him as the door was closing.

"See you at noon for lunch, Deidra," he said. I looked back at him and his crooked grin that made women swoon. The doors closed, and I couldn't reply because the office was full of people, and I'd made it a habit of keeping my business out of the gossip mill that ran through all of the cubicles at Nash Entertainment and Associates.

I walked over to my assistant's desk, waiting for her to finish her call. She smiled and hung up the phone, picking up the green tea from our favorite coffee shop. I didn't have time to battle caffeine withdrawals, so I decided to give it a try. She shook her head at me when I lifted my brow, indicating there were no calls I needed to return, so today shouldn't be crazy.

As one of three females at Nash Entertainment, I made a promise to myself to stand out and to make partner. I'd been working here for over ten years, and now that I was thirty-two years old, I needed to mind my p's and q's to make that happen. Increasing my billing hours and working late put two other team members and myself in the running for partner. The problem was that one of my competitors was the boss's son, and I didn't want it to be handed to him based on nepotism.

Mr. Nash promised his final decision would be based on who brought in the most clients and closed the top cases. I worked with a few B-list celebrities, but, overall, the majority of my clients were corporate businesses like sports teams and agencies. Brian Nash started Nash Entertainment and Associates thirty years ago. He was a formidable lawyer in the courtroom, known for getting his clients out of any significant lawsuits, and during college, when he came to speak about entertainment law at USC, I knew then I wanted to be the female version of him.

Lillian, my new assistant, opened the blinds in my office and turned the lights on, taking my coat and purse to hang it up. "Good morning, Deidra; how are you?"

"I'm good, Lillian. Can you check and let me know what I have going on around lunchtime?" I inquired.

Typically, I'd work through lunch, unless it was Bianca or Savannah and I meeting to catch up. Now that Savannah was a mom and working at her interior design firm, Houser Designs Inc., we didn't get to spend nearly as much time hanging out.

"Your calendar shows a hair appointment, but you had it done two days ago, so this must be code for something else," Lillian teased with an arched eyebrow.

"Why did I hire you again?" I questioned, sitting down at my desk, turning on my computer, and reading through emails.

"You're glowing." Lillian sat down in the chair in front of my desk.

"What?" I muttered, smoothing over my dress, touching my hair.

She grinned. "He must be special because, based on the last six months I've worked for you, men aren't exactly busting down your door. So he must be something special."

"I'm not in a relationship," I insisted.

Lillian continued peering at me with a glint of amusement dancing in her eyes. She was a perky, always smiling southern girl from Mississippi, twenty-five years old. If it weren't for her sweet, humble personality, I'd say she reminded me of myself when I first came to Los Angeles, looking to explore. I gained more insight out of life after moving from Ohio and coming here for college. In high school and college, I was the person who floated between the popular crowd and the nerds. I was athletic, but still curvy, and able to run track well enough for a scholarship that got me into USC to study law. Boys weren't my priority, but I did have some guys wanting to be number one in my life. Standing at five-seven, athletic and slim with a nice shape, medium-length curly hair, full lips, sharp cheekbones, and aquiline nose, I probably looked like the singer and model Ciara.

"I don't have a boyfriend, Lillian. Law is my boyfriend."

"Are you telling me there's not one guy in LA that you would date?"

"No," I stated resolutely.

My phone buzzed, and I answered, ignoring her constant barrage of questions. "Deidra Simmons," I said as I passed Lillian my client's file. We had a meeting in fifteen minutes, so I hoped this phone call wouldn't last long.

"What are you wearing?"

"I'm sorry I think you have the wrong number."

"You hang this phone up, and you will regret it, Deidra Simmons."

My brows furrowed at his tone. He knew how to get under my skin, and I allowed him to have the advantage because that devilish tongue of his kept me coming back. That's right. I was a virgin who loved oral sex, and I wasn't planning on going all the way with any guy until I was married.

With pursed lips, I responded sassily, "Please enlighten me on how I would regret hanging up on you?"

"You're still on the phone with me, so obviously I have your attention," he answered arrogantly.

Shaking my head, I replied, "I have a meeting to attend in fifteen minutes, so let's just cut to the chase. How can I help you, Mr. Nash?" The arrogance exuded through the phone.

"They can wait. I need the file on the Cromwell case," Logan said smoothly.

Logan Nash was the son of Brian Nash and the same asshole who stopped the elevator to intrude on my peace on this beautiful morning. I knew it sounded crazy to hate someone for always being handed everything in his life and, at the same time, be inexplicably attracted to them...but here I was.

Logan, of course, was at the top of his class at Harvard, played basketball, and slept with anything with a cute face and big butt, but in his father's eyes, he was a constant source of disappointment because he played and partied more than he maintained his business acumen, which is part of the reason he wasn't handed the position of partner. It was also why we had three months before the board meeting to vote on the next partner after Andrew a former partner, quit when he freaked out in court and lost a big case for the firm. Nash ended up getting sued because of it and had to pay close to two million in restitution, and Andrew left to work at his parents' accounting firm.

My mood veered sharply to anger. "The Cromwell case is mine."

"Deidra, as of eight o'clock this morning, it's my case. If you'd like to take this up with my father, he'll be in around noon today." The smug tone he gave off was evidence he was more than likely smirking on the other end of the phone.

"I will send the Cromwell case to you when hell freezes over, and Mr. Nash is more than capable of contacting me if a case was reassigned to another attorney," I said, and with that, I immediately hung up the phone and texted Savannah.

Me: *You wouldn't believe what that asshole just tried to pull.*

Savannah: *?*

Me: *Logan Nash.*

Savannah: *Isn't he the one....*

Before I finished reading the rest of her message, someone knocked on my door. "Come in."

Logan's assistant, Barbie, walked inside, wearing her usual short dress to try and get someone to notice her enough to catch a husband. She'd been an assistant to two out of the three lawyers on my floor. As soon as one fired her, she found herself with another one because her father was one of the board members.

"Logan sent me to grab the Cromwell case file." Barbie held her hand out, expecting me to hand the file over.

"I'm sorry he sent you on a pointless errand, but that case belongs to me, and I'm not turning it over unless Brian Nash personally tells me I need to step aside," I replied.

"Your funeral." Barbie popped her lips and swished her non-existent hips out of my office.

I turned back toward my phone to see what else Savannah wrote.

Savannah: *Sleeping with him?*

Me: *In what sense?*

Savannah: *Uhmm, you and him getting it on.*

Me: *No, he just gives me head from time to time.*

Savannah: *You like him?*

Me: *No, and I have a meeting right now. Talk later.*

"Mr. Jennings is set up in the conference room," Lillian said, poking her head into my office as I stood and grabbed my notepad and welcome package we prepared for all new clients.

"Thanks, Lillian, did you get a chance to offer him coffee or tea?" I questioned, checking my makeup in the mirror next to my coat rack. The firm allocated a small budget for junior associates to decorate, and having a best friend who does interior design definitely came in handy.

"I did, and can I just say you look cute today with that light purple skirt and vintage jacket?" she said brightly, following behind to the conference room for my first meeting with Jennings Motorsports.

"Mark Jennings, it's nice to see you again." I was surprised again by this unpredictable man standing at the edge of the conference table next to Mark.

"Deidra, such a pleasure to see you again. Logan was telling me you might be held up after an intense phone call, so he was going through the welcome packet with me and introducing me to the team," Mark stated.

Logan seemed to enjoy being a bug that irritated me and played games. That cocky smirk displayed on his face had my skin tingly. Having the feel of his lips on mine drove me internally crazy, but I promised myself he wouldn't win at this cat and mouse game.

Putting on my best smile, I extended a hand to Logan, letting him know I was on to the plot of stealing my client.

"Logan, thank you for keeping my client company, but I'm here now. I believe Barbie is looking for you in your office."

He tightened his grip around my hand, massaging ever so slowly, staring intently at my lips. Lillian cleared her throat, and I removed my hand from his, gesturing toward the conference room door.

Chapter 2: Logan

I liked to get under her skin, probably more than I should. I remembered when we made our first agreement, three years ago.

It was an office party on the twenty-fifth floor, and we could see the twinkling lights of the city buzzing with life just outside the window. Most of the team had already left for the night. She was talking with Geoffrey, the Junior Associate who had just transferred to the firm. I'd always had a crush on her, and seeing her in the skintight black dress with spaghetti straps and her hair hanging down, knowing what she was doing to every man in the building was driving me crazy. Me being my cocky self, I decided to walk over to where they were standing and stepped in between them, effectively interrupting their conversation.

"Excuse me, can I talk to you, Dee?"

"Logan, I've told you plenty of times my name is Deidra," she spat.

"Hey, we were talking; do you mind?" Geoffrey said snarkily.

"Amber in accounting is looking for you, something about the doctor's office needing to confirm your number before giving you your test results," I said, fucking with his chances of Deidra ever wanting him. I liked fucking with her, and calling her Dee instead of Deidra was one of many things I did, besides beating her to the punch on taking the best cases.

Geoffrey walked off, embarrassed. Deidra huffed and grasped my arm, pulling me into her office. "What is your problem?" she questioned.

"You."

"Me!" she screeched, rolling her eyes in annoyance.

I smirked, closing the space between us, grasping her waist and pulling her into a kiss.

"Mmmmm..." she moaned.

"I can tell it's been a while since you've had a proper orgasm based on your uptightness around the office."

"And what? You think you're the one who can provide me with that release?" Dee stated, crossing her arms over her chest.

"I can show you better than I can tell you," I challenged, running my tongue over my lips.

"If you want to be in rotation with the other men, all you've had to do is ask. I noticed you watching me, and I was waiting for you to get enough courage to speak up," Deidra taunted.

"Meet me in my office." I pressed a hand on the small of her back, whispering in her ear before planting a kiss and walking off.

This back and forth dance would come full circle tonight when I had her on her back, screaming my name.

A few minutes later, I entered my office, removing my tie, loosening my shirt and unbuckling my tie. Then I sat down on the couch, legs wide open and arms stretched out.

She came inside, stopping in front of me. "So?"

"Take off your underwear."

"This is a one-time thing and no penetration. Do I make myself clear?"

"Perfectly."

"We never speak of this again."

"Take off your underwear or slip off your dress."

"I mean, you seem like the type who catches feelings fast, and right now, my goal is focused on making partner, not getting involved with some corporate hotshot at work," she rambled on while removing her underwear. I grabbed them out of her hands when she sat next to me on the couch.

"Lock the door first."

"Okay."

I smirked, watching her getting flustered at my dominant commands.

She dropped her leg on the top of the table in front of me. Rising from the couch, I picked her up, laying her on the couch flat on her back, spreading her legs wide. I peppered the sensitive skin of her inner thighs with kisses.

"I need you to know that I'm a virgin, Logan..." she trailed off, squirming under me.

"I respect that and have no problem with you being a virgin." The sight of her bare, pliant body had me unbearably hard.

"We agree to leave this here."

My hands slid over her waist. Using my fingers, I spread her lower lips apart, flattening my tongue, swiping from the bottom to the top.

"Ohhhh!" she moaned.

"You have nothing to say now, huh?" I questioned.

"Shut up and keep going."

I reached up, squeezing her breast in her silk shirt. I stayed on my knees for two hours, fucking her with my tongue until she screamed and squirted in my mouth.

"Logan, aren't you looking extremely handsome today?" Olivia cooed as she walked into my office, perching on top of my desk and crossing her toned legs. She was wearing the shortest dress I'd ever seen, at ten in the morning. I'd brought Olivia in as a client a few weeks ago, and getting her to sign with me was a hard sell. She often flirted with me, and I told her on many occasions I wasn't interested. I mean, I have no problem with women taking control, but she was a little overzealous, throwing herself at me every chance we were alone. I leaned back in my chair, straightening my tie.

"Did you get my contract negotiations?" Olivia questioned.

"I did, and I think you need to be more reasonable. Some of these terms are pretty outrageous, Olivia," I replied, leaning back in my chair. I didn't want her getting any ideas, and she was too damn close right now.

"Well, maybe you can convince me to lower my demands with some one-on-one dinner and conversation."

Chapter 3: Deidra

Mr. Nash stood up while giving a speech to the final three candidates still in the running for partner. "As I'm sure you are all aware, I'm making my decision about a partner in a week. You've all brought in billable hours, which I do take into account above everything else. Also, the way you work in the office and how the team responds to you are important. The board votes, but ultimately, it's my decision as the owner of Nash Entertainment and Associates. Any questions?"

I looked over at Logan. He shook his head no. I was desperate for this position ever since I came to this law firm; this promotion was the reason I worked fifteen-hour days, sometimes showering and sleeping in my office if I had a case that needed more of my attention. Bringing in high priority clients to impress Mr. Nash was what helped to propel me further in the running.

"Sir, are we allowed to state our case before the decision is made? I can only speak for myself, and I want to make sure the playing field is fair. Lately, my clients have been poached, though I'm not saying it was done intentionally."

"Then exactly what are you saying, Miss Simmons?" Mr. Nash quipped.

"I think she's directing that toward me. I can assure you that my father hasn't stepped in to get my billable hours up or manipulated in my favor. I know it's hard to believe, but I do work hard, Dee," Logan explained, tapping the pencil against his notepad.

I narrowed my eyes at him.

"Is there something going on between you two?" Mr. Nash asked.

"No," we both spoke up at the same time.

"Good, keep it that way because I'd hate to have to let one of you go over having a relationship at work," Mr. Nash informed us.

"Dad, isn't that how you met Mom?" Logan joked.

"That's different, and it was a different time then."

"Mr. Nash, Logan and I only have a working relationship and nothing more," I said, standing up, grabbing my things and getting ready to leave.

Mr. Nash nodded and walked out of the conference room, leaving us alone. Logan stared at me as I picked up my bottled water and file folder to walk out.

"Why are you running?" Logan questioned.

"What?"

He took the bottled water out of my hand, along with the folder, and placed them on the table.

"I asked, why are you running, beautiful? You left without saying goodbye the other night." Logan started caressing my cheek.

"Stop, you know we can't do this at work."

"Fuck them. I want to know why you bailed on me."

"When did we start questioning each other? I'm not married, and there's no boyfriend in my life, so your question seems funny to me."

He pushed me up against the wall with both hands on the side of my face. "You're scared," Logan sensed, smirking and running his tongue across his lips.

"Stop being childish."

"Come over, I want you to see my place."

"No, we only hang out at hotels; you know this. Keeps things on neutral ground without any real feelings getting involved if we know where each other lives."

"That's bullshit, Dee, and you know it." He sighed in frustration.

"I have plans with Savannah and Bianca tonight."

"Cancel."

"Logan, are you still in here? I need your signature on this file." His assistant walked into the room. "Am I interrupting something?"

"No, we just finished up." I walked around him to grab my water and file folder as she glared at me. I headed back to my office, embarrassed by the encounter. As I walked inside, Lillian followed behind.

"Boss lady, here are your messages and your lunch," she said.

"Thanks."

"How did the meeting with Mr. Nash go? Did you tell him about the Cromwell deal?" she questioned, reminding me of what I needed confirmation on before he decided to give my highest performing client over. That was my case, and if Logan was trying to usurp it, there would be hell to pay.

"Thanks for reminding me, Lillian. I completely forgot to talk with him about the case. Do I have anything coming up after my lunch?"

"A few phone calls, but mostly you're in for the day."

"What do you have for lunch?" I queried.

She held up her barbeque salad and lemonade out of the bag.

"I think he's going to give it to Logan," I said, sighing in frustration.

"You can't think like that, Deidra; everyone on the floor and in this building knows you deserve to make partner. Your record speaks for itself."

"Logan has just as many clients, if not more. Plus, he does a lot of non-profit and charity work in the community."

"Maybe you should go out and do something at the local boys and girls' club?"

"And get my three-hundred-dollar Jimmy Choos messed up? I think not."

"Okay, how about you donate your time at the local college's tutoring center?"

"I'm not a babysitter, Lillian."

"Then you can forget about the partnership, Deidra," she said casually.

"You weren't this talkative when you first came here," I retorted as I rolled my eyes at her then stuck my tongue out. She burst out in laughter when a knock on my door interrupted us.

"I hope I'm not disturbing you ladies," Mr. Nash said, walking inside.

"Not at all, sir." I watched as Lillian stood up and grabbed her lunch to head back to her desk while I gestured for Mr. Nash to have a seat in the chair in front of my desk.

"After the conversation we had in the conference room, I wanted to follow up and make sure all parties are clear on what the expectations are at my firm."

"Okay."

Mr. Nash slid his hands in his pockets. "Deidra, you came to my firm ten years ago. You were bright, charming, a real go-getter, hungry. Your tenacity was just one of the reasons I chose you to intern, and eventually, you became an associate."

"Let's be honest, Mr. Nash, you lost an argument in the mock trial with me, and you felt embarrassed, so you had no other choice than to grab the young fresh lawyer out of law school. I remember you said it was like looking in a mirror," I replied.

He grinned. "Good memory, Miss Simmons. As Logan so elegantly stated, his mother and I met at the firm, and we started dating, then fell in love, and the rest is history."

"What are you trying to say, sir?" I questioned as I sat back in my chair and clasped my hands together.

"Logan is business-minded and sharp when it comes to being a lawyer. When it comes to relationships, he's not as wise."

"Are you calling your son a whore?" I joked.

"Unfortunately, yes, he's always with some new woman, and I'd rather you not get involved with him. You have a bright future ahead of yourself."

"You don't have to worry about that; Logan and I are just friends. Work buddies."

"I wouldn't want you to get hurt and have to come in every day looking at the person who caused you pain. My son is quite the rolling stone. "

"No worries, I have my eyes glued to the future, which I hope includes me as a partner," I replied.

"Nice try, but I haven't made my decision yet."

"Oh, I wanted to talk to you about the Cromwell case. Did you assign it to Logan?"

"The way his original deal was presented to me, I thought it was best to have Logan oversee things, but I know you've worked hard on scoring him as a client, so you have my blessing to keep the case."

"I'd already planned on doing just that," I answered.

Chapter 4: Logan

Two weeks later

Deidra finally accepted my request for a date. It was time for me to convince her I make time for what I want and the people who matter. I was having dinner with Dee at Mason's, a new vegan Italian restaurant that just opened.

She was wearing a light blue deep-plunging V-neck dress. Her hair was pulled up in a high ponytail, showing off her stunning cheekbones to perfection.

"You smell good, baby." I kissed the top of her hand.

"Thank you, so what's the occasion for dinner tonight?" While she had always stated that she wouldn't get involved in a relationship with me, I had other plans for Deidra. Asking her to dinner was step one in my plan to make her fully mine.

"I know we are competitors right now at work, but you've taken a step forward with letting me take you out, and I would like to have you come over to my place."

"Where do you live?"

"I live in a penthouse over in Century City, a property I invested in and hopefully will one day be the home for my future wife and kids," I explained.

"How much do they go for?"

"Mine was about a million, give or take."

"Wow, well, I'll stick to my little one-bedroom apartment. Keep it simple."

"Have you talked with your family lately?"

"I talked with my mom and told her about me going for partnership. She's excited, even if she has no clue the amount of work it's taken me to get here. How does your family feel about you seeing me?" she questioned as she took a sip of wine.

"My parents don't care about who I date as long as I commit to one person. I can't say I've been a poster boy for being a one-woman type of man until you came into my life."

"Logan, funny seeing you here," Olivia said, running her hand across my back and kissing my cheek as she walked up to our table.

"Olivia, you know Deidra, right?" I pulled back out of her reach, keeping a respectable amount of distance between us.

"Debbie, sure, how are you?" Olivia asked with a fake smile clearly pasted on her face. I could see from the look on Dee's face that Olivia deliberately screwing her name up had ticked her off.

"I'm fine," Deidra responded.

"Have you thought about my proposition, Logan?" Olivia inquired.

"Umm, do you not see we're on a date? Any business can wait," Deidra asked.

"Dee, it's okay. Olivia, we can talk tomorrow," I suggested.

"Why can't I join you two for dinner? Then we can go back to the office and look at those numbers," Olivia queried, motioning for the server to add an additional chair to the table.

"Olivia, I'm on a date."

"Don't you two work together? I know Mr. Nash doesn't allow employee fraternization. I'd hate for him to fire your little friend here," Olivia questioned in an attempt to manipulate the situation.

I watched as Deidra rolled her eyes and hid the smirk that was fighting to break free. If push came to shove, I would lay odds on Dee taking Olivia down.

"Olivia, you are my client, and what I do outside of business hours has nothing to do with you. I'm more than happy to meet with you in the morning, and we can discuss you wanting to buy the music studio, but right now, I'm busy."

As the server headed toward our table with our drinks, Olivia glared at Deidra before walking off.

"She wants you," Deidra commented bluntly.

"Not my type."

"Yeah, right."

The server arrived at our table. "Have you decided what you'd like this evening?" he asked after setting our drinks down.

"Can we have the lasagna and garlic bread, as well as another bottle of white wine?" I requested. The waiter nodded and left, and I returned my attention to Deidra.

"What's your type? Because from what I saw, she's blonde, slim, and rich," she sassed.

"I'm sitting next to my type. Olivia is just a client who has a rich family, and she is looking to get into the music business. Her parents are paying me a lot of money on top of what Olivia is paying me to help with overseeing the opening of a new music studio exclusively."

"All about the money with you," Deidra said quietly, taking another sip of her wine.

"Why are we talking about her when we should be focusing on each other?"

"You're right, and I'm glad you invited me to dinner because I want to make sure we're on the same page with things. Our little arrangement has to end."

"Why?"

"Because soon one of us will be a partner, and that wouldn't look right, and having the rest of the office think I'm a slut who slept her way to the top is not on my bucket list of achievements."

"Dee, you're overreacting."

She arched a brow. "You can say that because you're a man. Women in the workplace have the most pressure, and you being the boss's son doesn't help at all."

"No."

"What do you mean, no?" she snapped in a harsh tone.

"I don't agree with stopping our little arrangement."

"Logan, you have no choice."

I peered into her eyes before I grasped her hand and placed it on my lap, against the strain in my pants. "You feel that?"

"We're in public, Logan, and we shouldn't be doing this." Her mouth hung open in shock that I would be so brazen in a public place where anyone could see us.

"This is how you have me every day, all day. Your smile, your annoying attitude when you get pissed off at me for stepping on the elevator and disrupting your alone time. The scent of your perfume or the way you have your hair up showing off your cheekbones and perfect, full lips. Dee, I can't stop, and deep down, you don't want me to stop," I protested.

"Stop calling me Dee," she pouted.

"I'm the only person who can get away with calling you Dee, and you love that about me," I voiced.

Chapter 5: Deidra

He was the devil my mother told me to stay away from: the charming, slick-talking, dressed in suits and smelling like the Old Spice cologne you could only dream about. The hustle and bustle of the Century City neighborhood greeted me, luxury cars parked in the circular driveways in front of the building waiting for the valet to come, each building displaying lavish glass designs on the outside exterior. I could only imagine how high up the building went since he lived on the penthouse floor.

Once my Uber driver left, I let out a heavy sigh as I stood in front of his luxury high-rise condo that spread out over seventy-five acres of prime real estate and made my little apartment seem like a shoebox. Logan thought I was one of those women he could talk sweet to and make me fall in love, but nothing of the sort was coming out of Deidra Simmons' mouth.

The doorman greeted me with a head nod, holding the door open for me, and I strolled to the elevator, hitting the penthouse floor. I was wearing my best dress that always had men falling all over themselves. The red bustier dress against my mahogany brown skin and five-inch heels showcased my long, toned legs. I'd purchased it from one of my favorite designers that catered to women with curves. I had planned on going out after this with Savannah and Bianca to celebrate Savannah's opening of a second office and me closing on the Cromwell deal. I tightened my black silk shawl around my shoulders, clutched my purse, and stepped onto the elevator as the butterflies in my stomach fluttered.

As the sound of the elevator confirmed, I had made it to the top, and the doors opened. I was greeted with a wide door labeled P, which I assumed signified the penthouse. He must have been a significant person to have his entrance and emergency exit on the side. I knocked twice as I grew nervous and a shiver ran up my spine. My nipples hardened in anticipation of finally confronting him without anyone interrupting us.

The door opened, and I was flushed with embarrassment when Logan appeared in front of me shirtless and without shoes, wearing only a pair of blue jeans and a wide grin. His muscles flexed, and I licked my lips in reflex. *Focus, Deidra, don't let him win,* I thought to myself.

"You look beautiful, Deidra," Logan said.

I had no intention of falling under his spell, and he showed no signs of relenting as he motioned for me to come inside. As I crossed the threshold, I felt a hand brush against my back before his hand reached around and pulled me to his chest. He trailed a kiss across my shoulder, drifting up to my ear.

"I didn't come here for this." I moved out of his hold, turning around and putting distance between us.

His mouth pulled into a sour grin. "Where are you going?" He ran his finger across my naked shoulder.

"Out with some friends. I wanted to speak with you because you are acting like an ass at work, and people are starting to talk."

"I highly doubt you're going out dressed like that with friends. Tell the truth, you have a date," Logan teased, striding toward me looking like a fucking panther: sleek, quiet, fast, and deadly when catching his prey.

"None of your business. I told you the rules in the beginning: it's imperative not to catch feelings."

Looking around the room, the floor-to-ceiling windows reflected a warmth that belied the modern and sophisticated style of the building itself. The end result was a majestic panoramic view.

"This is your first time here. The building is an all-glass structure composed of four crystalline quadrants crowned with a distinctively angled roof. One of the reasons I purchased the penthouse for two million is because of the exterior glass that creates a luminous and transparent façade. It has sharp angles and terrace enclaves that accentuate its dramatic silhouette. Each portion of the façade is composed of multiple panes of glass, each slightly angled away from the other to refract sunlight during the day. But it transforms into an illuminated beacon at night," Logan explained, placing his hand on the small of my back while he gave me a tour of his home.

The scenery was sleek, modern with off-white and black curtains, six-foot-high ceilings, and hardwood six-inch-wide plank floors. He had a low-profile sectional, and we entered the master bathroom designed with a dual vanity with oriental white polished marble countertops. My mind was blown seeing the backsplashes, the custom Italian built-in walk-in closet with Hansgrohe fixtures and Bianco marble floors, a freestanding oversized soaking tub with a floor-mounted spout and hand shower as well as a separate walk-in shower.

"How many bedrooms?" I asked, running a hand across the luxurious texture of the marble.

"Four, but I made one into my office, and the other two are guest bedrooms."

"It's beautiful," I voiced, pivoting to the right to give myself more personal space. The sexual tension in the air was thick after I cut off our little situation when I saw pictures of him out on the town. I had to admit I missed our little combative, tit for tat "relationship" that usually resulted in us falling into bed with his full lips conquering my body from the top of my head to my pedicured toes.

A muscle ticked in his jaw. He came close, looking down at me intensely. "I missed you," Logan said quietly, his eyes compelling, magnetic. It took several seconds for me to adjust.

"Logan, stop playing games; we both know this won't work. Last I checked you're more interested in the playboy lifestyle," I promptly said, folding my arms across my chest.

He hiked his eyebrow in surprise. "We both agreed, in the beginning, to keep things casual. You can't come in here and act as if I cheated on you. We're not together—those were your words, not mine."

I cleared my throat and said, "Friends then," before I extended my hand for a shake. A deep, weighted sigh sprang forth from his lungs as his large hands cupped my face and then slid behind my head into the warmth of my hair. As he pushed me back against the wall, I shuddered in his palms from the feel of his mouth. He caressed my shoulder, down my arms, until our fingers tangled together.

He pressed his hard dick against me. "Can I have you, baby?" He stepped back, staring deep into my eyes for confirmation that we'd be taking this next step together.

Deep down, I was fooling myself for running away from what could be, and letting other women come in and out as I stayed on the sidelines and watched. Logan was what I wanted in a man. Yes, he was arrogant, cocky, and sometimes stubborn. But he made me laugh, and we had the same ambitions and thoughts. Our *situationship* was a long time coming that it would transition into something stable, and now I would be delving into having a boyfriend.

"I'm not giving up on becoming a partner if it comes my way," I expressed, waiting to see if this would be a deal-breaker for him. I worked too hard to give up my goals for any man.

"I'd never expect you to give up your dreams. Deidra, I'd quit before that ever happened. Baby, I just want you; we don't even need to do anything. Stay tonight and have dinner with me." He began to run his lips down my neck.

"I want you to. All of you."

He leaned back and smiled. "I'll be gentle; I pledge my life on it." He locked his mouth to mine like he would breathe me into existence with the force of his emotions. In an instant, he moved me toward the bed, helping me out of my dress and shoes.

Savannah and Bianca would forgive me for skipping out on them. Before I could get another word out, he covered my mouth with his and kissed me until I was fully lowered on the bed. I was only wearing a thong since the dress came equipped with a built-in bra attached. Fingers curled around my hand, and I smoothed my other one over the sleek bulge of his shoulder.

"Have I told you how good you looked tonight?" Logan commented, burying his face in my neck.

"Actions speak louder than words," I murmured, wrapping my arms around his neck and pulling him on top of me. His hands splayed out over my breasts, and I saw the pleasure written all over his face.

"Show me, Logan," I whispered, opening my legs wider. I pressed a hand against his swollen girth.

"Don't play with me, Dee," Logan groaned, flicking his tongue against my nipple, fast and wet.

"Mmmmmm...yes."

"God...damn, baby." He kissed me deeply as his hands explored my body. He grabbed a condom out of the nightstand, opening it with his teeth. I helped to slide it down his thick length. Positioning himself at my entrance, his palm drifted to my thigh, lifting it around him. Slowly he pushed the tip in and out, getting me wetter. The pressure was intense.

"Ahhhh, baby...you feel so good."

"Tell me if it's too much, and I'll stop. I don't want to hurt you," Logan told me as he struggled to hold himself back.

I cried out as he took my breast into his mouth and gently teased my nipple with his tongue. The sight of us together was beautiful as he took his time to make this special for me. One of his hands drifted between us to where we were connected, and he dragged his thumb across my bundle of nerves.

"I'm ready; go deeper, baby," I urged, wanting to feel more of him as the tears pooled in my eyes. Taking my cue, he slid inside, filling me up.

Chapter 6: Deidra

"Logan!" I cried out and dug my fingernails into his back.

"Fuck!" Logan paused, branding my neck with his lips, breathing fire across my skin.

"Ohhhh."

He teased my lips with his teeth, nibbling them ever so sweetly before he nudged my legs further apart, stroking into and out of me slowly. I picked up his steady rhythm and arched my back as his thrusts continued.

"Goddamn, I knew you'd be tight; it feels like you're suffocating me."

"Logannnn, ughhh, God. " He sank into me as my legs clasped around him. My body seemed to splinter into a thousand shards of ecstasy. I craved the feel of his body enveloping me, driving deeper.

The headboard started banging against the wall as sweat trailed down his forehead and chest onto the sheets. His gaze never wavered from my face; he was solely focused on pleasing me.

"Shit!" Logan droned out, pounding into me as our orgasms soared into overwhelming bliss that I'd never experienced before.

"Ahhhh...fuck!" We both moaned out at the same time.

Logan fell on top of me, breathing hard. I kissed his shoulders as he flipped on his back, pulling me on top of him.

"How do you feel?" Logan questioned, running a hand gently against my cheek.

"Tired," I teased playfully.

He smirked, kissing my forehead and easing out of me slowly.

"Stay put." He stood from the bed, walking toward the bathroom. A few minutes later, he came out with a towel and wiped between my legs. The cool cloth helped to ease the soreness. Logan threw the towel on top of the nightstand and reached over to pull me into his arms.

"Go take a shower while I change the sheets. Then we can practice with you on top," he said, rubbing my ass.

"I can see you'll want to practice a lot of things for the rest of the night." I giggled as he ran a hand up my inner thigh.

"Mmmm, you have no idea."

"We have to work tomorrow, so I can't spend the night," I informed him.

"Dee, you're not leaving my bed in the middle of the night. You can be late or have something delivered for you to wear. Either way you want, but you're not running out of here," Logan demanded, pecking my lips.

"Logan."

"Dee. I let you run things for a while, but now that we've made things official, you need to respect my wishes. Even if we were at your place, I wouldn't leave you in the middle of the night after having sex with you for the first time. Baby, relax and take a shower. After you get out, come ride my face." Logan patted my thigh, motioning for me to take a shower.

I guess this compromise would be a new thing I'd have to get used to because Deidra didn't take orders.

...

The next day we woke up together, had breakfast, and traveled into work together. All eyes stared, and I couldn't help but feel like I did something wrong.

"Fuck what they think. Don't let it get in your head," Logan said.

I smiled, nodding at his statement as he held my office door open. Walking inside, I placed my briefcase and coat down on my desk.

"You two looked mighty cozy." Lillian grinned, standing at the door.

"Hey, I'll be there soon." I hoped she'd take the hint to leave.

"Sorry, boss lady, but Logan's client, Olivia, is looking for him."

"Damn, I forgot I did set up a meeting with her this morning," he replied.

"Well, kiss me and go take care of your client. I'd hate to keep you from making our money." Standing on my tiptoes, I scrunched his suit jacket, laying a long, mouth-watering kiss on his lips. He didn't think Olivia was interested in him, but I knew women. She was like any other single woman trying to catch a rich man.

"Call me before you go to lunch so we can do something together today."

"Okay."

I sat down in my chair, grinning at the fine specimen who had me up against the wall, in the shower, and on the floor, fucking my soul out of my body the last few days.

An hour later, I was sitting in the café across from work eating lunch with Savannah.

"Did you finish remodeling your office space at the second location?" I asked Savannah.

"I did, and you wouldn't believe who my new client is." She was eating a tuna wrap, and I had a chicken parmesan salad and sweet tea. Before I could answer, I saw Logan and Olivia standing outside the building talking. She had her arm wrapped around him, leaning into his body, looking very close and happy.

"What are you staring at?" Savannah followed my eyes outside the window.

"Every second, it's either his assistant pissing me off or his client trying to fuck him."

"Keyword here, *trying* to fuck him. You trust him, right?"

Shrugging nonchalantly, I replied, "I guess."

"You guess? Deidra, you slept with the man. I can remember you saying you'd wait for marriage, and the minute Logan came around, everything fell to the wayside. So what changed?"

"Nothing."

"I'm gonna need a little more than 'nothing,' seeing as how you're gripping that butter knife ready to stab someone's eye out, or maybe their heart. You like this guy?"

"Who invented feelings? I mean my life was fine before I made that agreement with him three years ago. Now I've slept with him, and my mind can actually see us having kids. Me of all people, having kids! The only things I've ever wanted in life were a private jet when I made partner and the ability to travel the world. Love never looked like it was for me, so I never invested my time in men. I literally just let them eat my pussy, and it was only probably about three or four guys who ever did that, and he was the only one who made me cum," I confessed.

"He did a number on you. Cassian had me feeling the same way. He was an asshole and eventually wore me down, and we ended up married with a kid. Don't fight whatever is happening because plans can change on a dime."

"What if he likes her?" I asked, my tone alone admitting I was feeling vulnerable and weak, knowing she could take him from me.

"Based on what you've told me about Logan Nash, that man is head over heels in love with you. Take my advice and relax, let things progress naturally, and focus on what you can control," Savannah insisted.

Chapter 7: Logan

I pulled into traffic after work, headed to hang out with my friends at the club tonight. I finished meeting with my clients early, and Deidra wasn't answering my calls, so I figured she was slammed with work. I wanted to invite her back over to my place and test out the showerhead I had installed. Suddenly the Bluetooth in my car rang, and spotting Deidra's number across the screen, I answered.

"Dee, you missing me already?" I heard rustling in the background and cursing, which caused alarm bells to start blaring in my chest.

"Dee, you all right?" I questioned urgently.

"I'm fine, and I hit my foot against the desk. I was calling to check and see if you heard from your father. He said the decision would be made tomorrow," Deidra said.

"I know, and I'd like to know what your plans are after he makes the announcement if it doesn't go your way?" I stopped at the red light.

"I worked my butt off to get this position, and your father has to see that. I'm not saying you haven't put in the hours like me. But I want me more."

Turning in front of the nightclub, I parked and stepped out, handing my keys to the valet.

"Where are you? It's pretty noisy."

"I'm meeting some friends for a drink," I answered.

"Okay."

"What does that mean?"

"It means just what I said."

"Dee, don't start. I'm only having drinks. You never had a problem with me hanging with my friends before." The bouncer let me inside, and I walked straight up to the VIP section that Jacob texted me earlier to meet him at. Jacob's an NBA player who hired me as his lawyer, and we've been friends ever since.

On top of big businesses, I have a few celebrity clients. It's one of the reasons I know making a partner is the next step in my goals. I didn't have the luxury of my parents giving me anything besides paying for college. I worked my ass off and built my career from the ground up, and having the Nash last name could be a good thing or bad depending on who you were talking with. Dee didn't see how my father only really dealt with me if it could bring him money or benefit him in some way. As the only child, I had to fight to get attention from him where he would be proud of me for doing something besides making him richer. The love of law had been in my blood for years.

Jacob tapped me, and I sat next to him and his entourage. It was like that TV show back in the day.

"You finally got away from the desk?" Jacob joked.

"Who's your friend, Jacob? He's cute." A random groupie tried to sit in my lap.

"Call me when you're free," Deidra said, hanging up before I could get another word in. I sighed in frustration as the bottle girl came over to pour champagne for everyone.

"This is a celebration. I signed on for another three years with Storms, and you brokered a deal worth a hundred million, my friend," Jacob said, clinking glasses with the crowd.

"Hey, you want some company tonight?" the groupie shouted over the music.

"I'm good," I replied, motioning for the girl to move over so I could have a conversation with Jacob. Jacob must have seen the look on my face because he jerked his head, and the groupie moved away from us.

Once she was gone, he leaned closer and said, "Man, I wanted to talk to you about your penthouse. I'm looking for a permanent place, but not a house yet. I heard great things about your area."

"Come by and check it out this week. Starting price is around a million and can go upwards of two, so make sure you are serious about moving in and not bullshitting. The types of people who live there are high profile, like you and me. At the same time, it's peaceful, and having a string of women coming in and out won't work," I informed him as I glanced around the group of women making out in front of us.

The sight of women making out did nothing for me now. Even though Dee and I had been pussyfooting around being together for years, I had grown tired of the fast and easy lifestyle and longed to be with her. Right now, though, I knew she was upset with me because of what she heard, and she was worried about making a partner. Damn, I needed a fix of her magic pussy to put me to sleep.

"I understand. Put in a good word for me, will ya? How is your girl doing?" Jacob questioned, taking a drink out of the glass he held in his hand.

"Not happy I'm out with you." We both chuckled at my response. The bottle girl came back upstairs to hand us another round of drinks.

"Come dance with me?" The blonde, petite female who offered to go home and keep me company extended her hand for me to take.

"Not tonight, love. I'm relaxing with my friends." Checking the time and seeing it was past midnight, I decided to call it quits. I had an early day tomorrow, and staying out too long would cause even more drama.

"I'm heading out. Jacob, make sure you call me tomorrow so I can set up a meeting for you to tour the property." We slapped hands, and I walked off, heading out of the club as the crowd started to get even rowdier.

Forty minutes later, I stuck my key in the door of my penthouse, shutting the door behind me and kicking off my shoes. Stretching, I loosened my tie and walked toward my bedroom.

Opening the door, I noticed Dee lying in bed with the covers below her waist. Removing my shoes, shirt, and pants, I slid in behind her. I wrapped my arms around her waist and pulled her back into my chest.

"You have fun tonight?" she mumbled.

"Go to sleep," I grunted out after her elbow jabbed me in the side of my stomach.

She got out of bed, huffing and puffing.

"Excuse me. I wasn't the one out late partying with some bimbo," Dee complained, her hands on her hips and her lip poked out.

"Do you trust me?" I questioned.

"You're a man, so my trust is minimal for the time being," Deidra jokes.

I stepped out of bed and lifted her chin, kissing her lips, staring deep into her eyes. "I'm only invested in you."

Chapter 8: Logan

"Logan, I have your files for you to look over," my assistant stated. In twenty minutes, my father was calling the board in to have the final vote on partnership. I made sure to dress up in my best suit and tie combo to impress the old man.

"Thanks and have you seen Deidra today?" I questioned.

"No, I haven't; is there something you need? I'm more than capable of handling anything you might require."

"I'm good. Can you get lunch ordered for two people? After the vote today I think we will both need something to cheer us up. Make sure to order the best bottle of wine."

"What about your meeting with Jacob later today?"

"Cancel it or have him meet with my realtor on his own. I think Deidra and I need a little alone time."

"Is she your girlfriend?" my assistant asked, folding her arms and glaring at me.

"If she is, what's the problem?"

"Nothing."

Just then my phone rang, and I picked it up, hearing my dad's assistant requesting my presence in the conference room. Leaving the files on my desk, I looked in the mirror, checking my face for any blemishes, and popped a breath mint in my mouth. Then I headed out the door. I noticed Deidra walking with Lillian, laughing about something.

"Let me grab the door for you, ladies," I stated, gesturing for them to go ahead of me.

I nodded at all the board members in greeting as I walked inside and found an empty seat. My father was standing with his assistant at the head of the table as Lillian and Deidra took their seats.

"Thank you all for coming. Today has been a year in the making, and I didn't want to make you wait any longer. As you know, Nash

Entertainment and Associates are bringing on another partner, someone who has shown they've been on top of not only keeping our clients happy, but also bringing in billable hours, putting us on the path to become the top law firm in the country. I just want you to know that after much deliberation, the board has made a decision, and I agree with that decision wholeheartedly."

I looked over at Deidra, and she held Lillian's hand in comfort.

"Logan, welcome aboard as a partner. You'll not only have a new office, but the top pick of any cases you want, and use of the private jets and corporate credit cards."

"Congratulations, Logan!" The board clapped and cheered as Deidra sat stone-faced. A part of me was happy and sad that only one of us would have the opportunity to get ahead. We'd both been at the firm for a long time.

"Deidra, it was a hard choice, but I hope you understand I didn't make it on a whim," Dad said, reaching his hand out for a shake. She put on a brave smile and captured his hand before standing up and leaving the room. I was about to follow behind her when he called my name.

"Son, hold up a second."

"Yeah."

"Give her some space; she's still in shock, and seeing as you're my son, she'll probably take her frustrations out on you."

"Did I earn this on my own, or did you hand it to me because I'm your son?" I wondered.

"What kind of question is that? You should know better than anyone I don't do favors for anyone, especially for family members. Even if you weren't my son, I would still give you the partner position because you earned the right to have the title. I know the time you've put into your career and the long nights working late. I'm not completely oblivious to you trying to get my attention, growing up in my shadow. Your mother and I didn't want you to depend on us or the Nash name. Like I said, give her some time, and she'll understand," Dad said as he clapped a hand on my shoulder and walked away. Deidra wasn't up for lunch after the vote, so let my assistant keep the food.

...

Four hours later, I was home mapping out my client list and who I could keep on and who would be better off with junior associates. Now that I had the partnership, I needed to represent only the best of the best. Hearing a knock on my door, I figured it was the doorman with the food I ordered. Standing up, I went to the door in nothing but my jeans and no shirt since I was at home.

"What are you doing here?" I asked Olivia.

"I came to bring you your contracts for my new deal."

"You didn't need to bring them all the way over here."

"I know, but I like to make sure my lawyer is well equipped and taken care of in every way." Olivia flirted, running her index finger down my chest suggestively. Right when I was about to remove her hand, Deidra appeared at the door.

"Sorry for interrupting. I'll call next time before dropping over."

"Deidra, wait," I shouted, watching her run back toward the elevator like the devil himself was nipping at her heels. Olivia sat on the edge of my couch, smirking.

"Logan let her go; she's not worth chasing after. I like your place; it's like a museum." I glared at the woman acting like something was between us. Her attempts at flattery were useless since she couldn't see much of anything.

"I need my shoes and keys."

"Why? Listen, how about I order us some food, and then I can help you with your work."

"Get out."

"What?"

"Get out! I don't need your help. I didn't say anything before because you're my client, but all the little flirting and underhanded comments at work about us being a great team outside of client and lawyer didn't go unnoticed. However, I would never go there with you because Deidra is my girlfriend, and you were my client."

"But you've never committed to any one woman, everyone in the office knows that. I can be discreet." Olivia stepped closer, kissing me on the lips.

I gripped her by the arm, pushing her toward the elevator. "Find someone else to play these games with, Olivia. I'm not your sugar daddy or anything else to you." I escorted her toward the door, then slammed it in her face.

I grabbed my phone to call Deidra to come back. Seeing me shirtless probably had her thinking something was going on. After picking up a shirt to head downstairs, I continued to try calling her cell. The first call went to voicemail, as did all the others I made that night.

After twenty minutes of looking around the lobby I went back up to try and drink the bullshit away.

Chapter 9: Deidra

"I have the wine." Savannah came inside and hugged me before going toward the kitchen.

"I ordered pizza, tacos, and burgers," I said.

"Are you having a party or dealing with a breakup?" Bianca queried.

I lay across the couch face-down. "I hate men," I mumbled under my breath.

Bianca slapped me on the ass to sit up. "Have you showered today?"

I smelled under my arms, then replied, "What's the point?"

"Honey, I know how you feel. Maybe give him a call and talk things out. Maybe nothing happened between them, and you're overreacting for nothing."

I shook my head. "He was shirtless; his pants were undone, and his client was dragging her dragon hands down his chest."

"Were his pants down around his knees? I mean you said she was clothed, so maybe she'd just arrived at his place."

"I refuse to be with a cheater. I gave that man everything, and he promised to be faithful."

"Deidra, I think you're pissed about not making a partner and taking it out on him when, in reality, nothing probably happened."

All of a sudden, my phone rang. I picked it up and noticed my mom calling. "Hey, Mom."

"Are you still moping over that boy?" Mom fussed.

"Ma, it's not that simple. I work with him and the slut he cheated with."

"Watch your mouth, Deidra. Are Savannah and Bianca there with you?" Mom asked.

"Hi, Miss Rhonda!" Savannah expressed, taking the phone out of my hand.

"Deidra, take it from me: you need to talk with him and let him explain the situation before you write him off," Bianca insisted.

"Is that what Denton did for you?"

"We decided to stay friends because our careers are taking us in different directions, and I wouldn't want to hold him back. Tonight isn't about me. We're here to help you get your mind right after we overeat some food."

"I miss him."

"Ohh, boo, you miss the dick, not the man. Once he laid the pipe, your entire world opened. Trust me, I get it, more than anybody," Bianca jokes.

"Have you slept with Denton?"

She nodded her head sheepishly.

"Kick Wayne out of your life before it's too late, Bianca." I worried about my friend and the amount of stress she was under trying to move on and still deal with an ex that doesn't seem to care about her feelings or respect her as the mother of his child. Bianca could do so much better, and I hope she'll realize bigger and better things are waiting for her once she sees Wayne is in the past.

Chapter 10: Logan

One month later, Deidra had finally come back to the office after taking a few weeks off. She had Lillian screen all my calls, and at one point wouldn't allow me in her office. She was being childish, but I eventually wore her down, and now we were sitting at dinner with my parents, and once we had a long talk, she agreed to work things out.

I'd had food catered, and we sat in the dining room of my penthouse. The low hum of Beethoven played in the background.

"Deidra, I hear you've forgiven my son's bad behavior," my mom said.

During our talk, I told Deidra what had actually happened that night with Olivia and advised her that I had removed her from my client list. She was still with the firm, but another partner handled her now.

"It didn't happen overnight," Deidra insisted.

I grasped her thigh, leaned over and kissed the side of her cheek.

"I remember when your father and I had our first fight. You have to make him work to get back in your good graces, Deidra. I know my son and husband can be a little calculating with their emotions, and he made Logan partner over you. But if you are ever looking to branch out on your own, you'll have an investor in me. Women have to stick together," Mother expressed, taking a sip of her wine.

"Honey, whose side are you on?" Dad questioned.

"I'm on the side of my son, but at the same time, I think you should open another partner position at the firm for Deidra," Mother advised.

"It doesn't work like that, Mildred. These votes come up every five years for a reason. In time, Deidra will get to that place," Dad stated.

"Everything happens for a reason," Deidra said, taking a bite of her meatloaf.Dinner continued as we talked about plans for the law firm and Mom wanting me to come over more for dinner with Deidra. Twenty minutes later we helped to clean up the dishes. I put the dishes away as I watched mom and Deidra laugh at one of her stories about me taking the car without permission when I was younger and getting in trouble by running a stop sign and having the police show up to bring me back home. I wiped my hands off and walked up behind Deidra and kissed the back of her neck.

"Are you ready to go?" I queried.

"I'm having fun with your mom," Deidra replied, placing her hand on top of mine.I squeezed her close to my chest.

"Logan, please don't mess this up. I like Deidra for you." Mom commented.I chuckled at her statement.

"What about telling Deidra not to mess up? Know how long it took to get her to open up to me?" I asked.

"She had her reasons." Mom said.

"Deidra, what did you do to my mom?" I inquired.Deidra stepped out of my hold and turned around to face me.

"Nothing," Deidra said. Mom laughed and stood on her tiptoes and kissed my cheek.

"I can't wait for more family dinners."

"I bet. Can we go now?" I questioned.

"Yes, and be safe," Mom told.

"Tell Dad I'll call him later," I said, reached for Deidra's palm to walk out of the house. I opened the front door, Deidra grinned and greeted me on the lips and I smacked her on the ass. I gently pushed her up against the passenger side door and pecked her lips.

"Your beautiful baby," I said.

"Thank you, baby," she answered.I released her body, opened the passenger side door for her to get inside, and walked around to the driver's side door. I slid my seatbelt on, and started the ignition and turned the radio on to old school R&B with Patty Labelle, and Marvin Gaye. I gazed over at the woman I love and smiled to myself that she finally saw that we could be more. From the second, she came to the law firm I knew this would be my future and her smart mouth, sexy body; and spunky attitude that could bring any man to his knees. I was happy she chose me.

Chapter 11: Deidra

"Baby, right there."

I felt his warm lips under the covers as I grabbed the back of his head. Shifting my leg, I gave him more access as he pleased me with his finger and tongue.

"Ohhh, Logan," I moaned, pushing his head closer. Once I gave him my virginity, I'd been more into sex than him. I often woke him up with my head followed by riding his dick slowly, then switching to reverse cowgirl.

"Are you going to listen to me going forward when I tell you something?" he demanded, stopping his penetration with his tongue.

"Baby, stop playing."

"No, I want to see that ass up against the window. Come on, get out of bed, Dee." Logan reached over, picked me up, and I wrapped my legs around his waist as he entered me, gripping my ass as we both sighed from the pleasure of our bodies joined together. I playfully gripped the back of his head, biting his bottom lip.

"Make love to me, baby," I whispered in his ear. He draped a hand around my neck, squeezing gently.

We walked toward the living room, kissing, moaning, and grinding slowly. It was insane how safe he made me feel in his arms, and I knew I made the right decision to give my heart, mind, and body fully to our relationship. My stomach did a flip when my back hit the window. A chill went up my spine from the cold.

"I want you to taste me," he murmured, running a hand up and down my thigh and back.

The way he purred the words caused my body to tense and my lips to tingle with the urge to suck every drop out of his body. When he pressed my hand against his dick, I squeezed, then loosened my legs from around his waist to squat down in front of him. He ran a hand over my hair. This wasn't my first time giving him head, but now that we'd made things official, I wanted him to feel pleased as much as he pleased me. Removing my t-shirt, I let my breasts free, twisting my nipples and craning my neck to look up at him.

"Please me," he demanded.

He urged my lips apart, easing just the tip of his dick inside. Rubbing up and down his thigh, I moaned, sliding him down further. He paused, mouth agape while staring down at me. I ran my tongue down to the base of his balls, then pulled back. Popping his dick out of my mouth, I stroked him at a steady pace before I took his balls into my mouth. I smirked when I caught him observing me out of the corner of his eyes, knowing he was ready to bust.

"How does this feel?" I pushed my index finger underneath his balls between his pleasure point.

"Fuck, Dee, wait," Logan groaned, biting his knuckles.

"No." I closed my eyes then took him down my throat again, breathing through my nose. After he got past a certain point, I didn't have a gag reflex and was able to open up more, so I was able to please him longer.

"Get up!" Logan shouted, tapping my shoulder. I rose on my tiptoes, and he locked his mouth on mine. Picking me up, we rotated positions again, and he entered me fast, like he was on a mission and our lives depended on the next few minutes.

"Ughhhhhhh, baby."

Logan pounded a hand against the window. His thrusts became unhinged and out of control. He pulled my chin up so we could meet eyes.

"Fuck...this is forever, Dee. I swear, baby," Logan promised.

I was grateful he lived in a penthouse because our screams and moans rose higher and higher.

...

Two hours later, we had company over. I called Bianca, Savannah, and Cassian over to hang out after we made love, showered, and ordered food. The kids played in the pool area, and later we planned a movie in the screening room he had built.

"Deidra, you look happy." Bianca started nudging me in the arm.

I remembered my earlier activities and the reason for my smile. "I am happy."

"Did the talk go well with Mr. Nash and you?" Savannah asked.

"Honestly, I was disappointed, but everything happens for a reason, and Logan deserved the partnership as much as I did. I'm just glad he got Olivia transferred to another associate," I advised, shaking my head about having to fight that girl when she tried to sabotage me. That made me think about my conversation with Mr. Nash.

"Deidra, you're good at your job, and this is not a bad reflection on your performance."

"I get it, Mr. Nash. Logan's more outgoing than me and brings in the big dollars."

"That's true, and he's hungry for it. Take no prisoners. I need someone who will eat, breath and hustle by any means."

"I bring in the second highest roster of clientele," I answered.

"Yes, but the business and brand of Nash needs to be seen as a global firm. Most of your clients aren't very well off for the long term."

"Good. I can't believe you were thinking of leaving us. Our days would be terrible if we didn't have our daily dose of Deidra's crazy life." Savannah laughed.

"Logan said the same thing about me and always wanting to run when something doesn't go my way. He's challenging me, and I get along with his family fine."

The weeks I had spent away from the office when I didn't get the partnership had given me a lot of time to reflect on what I did and didn't want out of life. Logan had wisely stayed away to give me that time, and while I missed him horribly, him doing that showed me that there was far more to the man than I had realized.

When I finally admitted, at least to myself, that Logan Nash was something I wanted, I gave in and we talked. While I hoped to eventually branch out on my own with my own firm, right now, I was content to stay right where I was for the time being.

One of the best things that came out of it all was that Mr. Nash and the board abolished the "no fraternization" policy once he realized Logan was serious about pursuing me. We kept it professional at work, but once we were home, all bets were off.

Alesha ran over to Bianca with her juice bottle to get it and opened it for her. Denton was talking to Cassian and Logan in the kitchen.

"How are things with you and Denton?" I asked Bianca once Alesha had gone back to play.

"Slow, and he pays more attention to Alesha than me. I'm low key jealous." Bianca chuckled.

"You know the reason for that. Bianca, until you cut ties with your ex, Denton won't put his feelings on the line only to end up heartbroken if you take Wayne back," Savannah preached.

The guys walked outside toward us, and Logan kissed my forehead, putting his arm around my shoulder. Denton sat at the table staring at Bianca. Alesha came over and sat on his lap.

"Deidra, I know you're looking for more clients, and I might need a lawyer to represent me now that my other lawyer retired," Cassian chatted amiably.

"That would be great, Cassian. Wait, did Savannah put you up to this?" I inquired, not wanting a pity client. I was a damn good lawyer, but having my best friend force her husband to hire me out of some loyalty was not cool.

"Savannah didn't put me up to this, and I researched you. Before you say anything, Logan didn't put a bug in my ear, either. Nash Entertainment is a well-known firm, and a few of my clients have spoken highly about your legal prowess," Cassian explained.

"Okay, well, next week I'll be in your office at eight a.m., and we can talk about your plans and what I can bring to the table." He reached out his hand and shook mine.

The rest of the afternoon flowed easily with laughter and card games. I talked about my plans for moving in with Logan and what I envisioned were the next steps in my career. Later that night we were watching the full moon and feeling the cool breeze caress our skin. Looming over my height, he kissed the back of my neck, wrapping his arms around my waist.

"Thank you," I said, turning around and facing him.

"For what?"

"For not giving up on me, and for the extensive closet space," I joked with a wink.

He burst out in laughter. "Oh, so you're only in love with me because of my penthouse and closet space?" Logan teased, pecking my lips.

"That's not the only thing I'm in love with..." I allowed my hand to drift down to his crotch. I gripped his dick, slipping my tongue in his mouth. "Let's go to bed and test out some of my new moves."

Epilogue: Logan

Six months later, we stood on the balcony of our condo together, hugged up. Deidra stood in front, wearing a crop top and boy shorts. She tipped her face to the sun, and I wrapped my arm around her waist. I pulled her in close, smelling her sweet lemon-scented shampoo. We decided to stay home from work today and enjoy our engagement and her pregnancy. My parents wanted us to come over and visit, but I needed her close; getting alone time together was rare with our schedules.

"How are you feeling?"

She drew in a deep breath. "I'm fine, Logan. Stop stressing about the baby and me. The doctor said everything was just fine with the baby ." She turned around and leaned against the railing.

Unconsciously, my brow furrowed. "I'm not stressed."

"Yeah, right," she snickered, withdrawing from my arms and moving to the right, taking a strawberry off the table. I got up early to make breakfast so she could sleep in a little longer, and we'd have more time to talk and relax. Over the past several months, our relationship went from wanting to kill each other, to me dropping to my knees and proposing marriage. I realized the fast life wasn't for me anymore, and I wanted something more stable. She was my refuge from the pressure of trying to live up to what my father wanted. Even though I made partner at the law firm, and she left to start her practice, even though my mom invested in her dreams, we still managed to keep a steady schedule so that our nights belonged to each other, and we'd leave work at work.

"Do you know, ever since you found out I'm pregnant, you've contacted Savannah and Cassian about buying every pregnancy book to learn what to expect when expecting?" she questioned with an arched eyebrow.

She was smiling and radiant as she dipped the strawberry in the chocolate and fed me. I took a bite, licking the excess chocolate off her finger. All I could think about was watching her give birth to our first child and walking down the aisle to me in a long white dress and becoming my wife.

"I like to be prepared for anything, my love." I crossed my arms over my chest, watching the fullness of her cheeks. Her hips had spread a little with her pregnancy, but I loved having more to grip as I pounded into her tight, wet sheath.

The moment she gave me her virginity, I promised to cherish every inch, and I intended to keep my promise. Even though she was a virgin, Deidra was still experienced in other things, and when we decided early on to be friends with benefits, I learned every curve of her that turned her on. She more than satisfied me in the bedroom, and she never had to worry about competing with any other woman for my attention.

"What plans do you have for me today?" she asked.

Amusement flickered in my eyes, and she laughed. "I wanted to stay in bed with you and order food and watch some bad reality TV shows," I answered.

She laughed infectiously. "Baby, you don't have to torture yourself like that. We should get dressed and go shopping or something. I saw these new heels I'm dying to buy."

"No heels, remember?"

"Uhmm, I think pregnant women are fine to wear heels. Come on, please, Logan, take me out shopping?"

"Is this how it's going to be when we get married? You give me the puppy dog face and pout to get what you want?" I questioned.

Her wide-eyed innocence was merely a smokescreen. "Logan, do you know why I said yes when you proposed to me?" she asked.

"Why did you say yes, Deidra?"

She extended her hand to me, and I followed behind her toward our bedroom. The moment she moved in, she redecorated everything, and it was no longer a bachelor pad like she called it when I first brought her here. We ended up purchasing the next floor below us and opened up space for her to have her office and a spa room, along with expanding for the baby's room, since my parents already wanted us to have more kids. Deidra wanted to wait after her practice was established a little longer, however, and I agreed.

"Not only because of your charming face, but I fell in love with your home. It's like an extension of you and your personality, and the way you've only had me here and no other woman means a lot to me. This high rise sealed the deal, Mr. Nash."

"You're welcome, Mrs. Nash."

The End.

About the Author

KeKe Renée writes sinful, sexy, and spicy romances in novelette, novella, and short story form in genres ranging from erotic, paranormal, contemporary, and women's fiction with HFN or HEA.

Spotify

1. Meghan Stallion - Captain Hook
2. Nicki Minaj - The Night is Still Young
3. 112 Featuring Ludacris – Hot & Wet
4. Joe - I Wanna Know
5.Beyonce - Diva
6. Mary J. Blige - Take Me As I Am
7. Rihanna - Kiss It Better
8. Chris Brown - Take You Down
9. Usher - Climax
10. Usher - My Way

What's Next

Want to know what happens next?

Follow me on social media to catch the next release.

Reviews are the lifeblood of the publishing world. They're read, appreciated, and needed. Please consider taking the time to leave a few words on Goodreads, or Bookbub.

Sign up for updates and sneak peeks at the sites below.

www.bookbub.com/kekerenee

www.3[1]04pu[2]blishing.com[3]

www.goodreads.com/author/kekerenee

Facebook.com/304publishing[4]

www.Twitter.com/304_publishing[5]

www.Instagram.com/304publishing[6]

www.Facebook.com/autho[7]rkekerenee

www.304publishing.tumblr.com[8]

---

1. http://www.304publishing.com

2. http://www.amazon.com/author/chiquitadennie

3. http://www.304publishing.com

4. http://facebook.com/chiquitassteamyreadinggroup

5. http://www.twitter.com/304_publishing

6. http://www.instagram.com/304publishing

7. http://www.facebook.com/authorchiquitadennie

8. http://www.304publishing.tumblr.com/

304 Publishing Company

We showcase authors writing African American, Interracial, Women's Fiction, Urban Romance, Erotic, and Contemporary Romance novels. Along with Thriller, Suspense, Poetry, Beauty, and Style Books. Thank you for taking the time out to visit. Join our mailing list to stay updated with new releases and blog posts.

Catalog Releases

By Keke Renée:

Wet Heat

His Peace, Her Pleasure

Baby, It's Cold Outside

Love Don't Live Here Anymore, Books 1, 2

One Night Only-A Novelette

Cassian and Savannah Love By Design

Every Time We Touch (A Wet Heat Novelette)

By Chiquita Dennie:

Temptation

Antonio & Sabrina: Struck in Love, Books 1, 2, 3,4

Janice & Carlo: Captivated by His Love

Heart of Stone, Book 1: Emery & Jackson

Heart of Stone, Book 1.5: Emery & Jackson, A Valentine's Day Short Story

Heart of Stone, Book 2: Jordan & Damon

Heart of Stone, Book 3: Angela & Brent

By Ava S. King

Agent Red (Teagan Stone Book1)

Thank you so much for reading and if you enjoyed the crazy ride and decide to leave a review we'd truly appreciate the support.

His Peace
HER PLEASURE
KEKE RENÉE

love don't live here *anymore*

ANDREW SISTERS BOOK 1

KeKe Renée

Love
DON'T LIVE HERE
Anymore
(NOVELETTE)
(ISABELLA ANDREW BOOK 2 A NOVELETTE)
KeKe Renée

www.ingramcontent.com/pod-product-compliance
Lightning Source LLC
Chambersburg PA
CBHW071244130726
47998CB00003B/1046